TRADEWIND BOOKS

THE CLONE CONSPIRACY

Born and raised in Britain, Canadian writer Simon Rose now lives in Calgary, Alberta. His first novel, *The Alchemist's Portrait*, was published by Tradewind Books in 2003. *The Sorcerer's Letterbox*, published by Tradewind Books in 2004, has been short-listed for the Ontario Library Association 2005 Silver Birch Award for Fiction and the Diamond Willow Award, the Young Readers' Choice Award chosen by upper elementary students in Saskatchewan.

The
Consp

Clone
iracy

The Clone Conspiracy

by Simon Rose

VANCOUVER   LONDON

*This book is dedicated to
my parents and all my family in England.
- S.R.*

Published in Canada and the UK by Tradewind Books Ltd.
www.tradewindbooks.com

Distribution in the UK by Turnaround
www.turnaround-uk.com

Distribution in Canada by Hushion House
Orders should be placed with Georgetown Terminal Warehouses
orders@gtwcanada.com

Text copyright © 2005 by Simon Rose
Cover illustration © 2005 by Bob Doucet
Book design by Jacqueline Wang

Printed in Canada on recycled paper
10 9 8 7 6 5 4 3 2 1

Cataloguing-in-Publication Data for this book available from the British Library.

Library and Archives Canada Cataloguing in Publication

Rose, Simon, 1961-
The clone conspiracy / by Simon Rose.

ISBN 1-896580-80-7

I. Title.

PS8585.O7335C56 2005   jC813'.6   C2005-902339-2

*The publisher thanks the Canada Council for the Arts and
the British Columbia Arts Council for their support.*

 Canada Council   Conseil des Arts
for the Arts   du Canada   BRITISH
COLUMBIA
ARTS COUNCIL

*The publisher also acknowledges the financial support of the Government
of Canada through the Book Publishing Industry Development Program
(BPIDP) and the Association for the Export of Canadian Books.*

Contents

Prologue

At the dawn of the
twenty-first century,
governments around
the world banned
human cloning.
However, the genetic
genie had already
escaped from the
bottle.

1

Luke's Lesson

Luke searched for a sign of weakness in his opponent, but Patrick left him no opening. As Patrick's eyes narrowed, Luke stepped back and quickly blocked Patrick's kick. But the force of the blow knocked Luke back. Patrick lunged at him, but Luke recovered in time to throw a punch that Patrick easily avoided. In an instant, Patrick pulled Luke's leg out from under him and pinned him to the mat.

"Do you give up?" Patrick asked, grinning widely.

"Get off me," Luke said breathlessly.

"Okay, boys," the coach shouted. "That's enough. The lesson's over. See you next week."

Patrick helped Luke up, and they both headed off to change. The boys had taken karate since they were seven, but Patrick had always had a slight edge over Luke. And now Patrick was at least two inches taller and considerably stronger, so he usually won their weekly matches.

Once outside, the boys sat down on the sidewalk with their backs against the wall beside the gym.

"Beat you again," Patrick said. "Maybe when you've grown a little, eh?"

"Yeah, we'll see what happens next time. It's not about being bigger. Coach says it's just a matter of learning how to turn your opponent's strength against him."

Patrick simply smiled and wiped his forehead with the back of his hand. "Got any water left?" he asked.

"Sure," said Luke tossing him his bottle.

The sidewalk was crowded that afternoon with office workers trying to take advantage of the beautiful July day. Luke looked across the street and saw a dark-green car with blacked-out windows pull up. The passenger window opened, and a camera with a long lens pointed toward them. He was about to mention the camera to Patrick when a red minivan pulled up by the sidewalk in front of them.

"Mom's here," Patrick said, handing Luke the bottle back.

They both jumped up and sprinted for the front-seat passenger door.

"Hey, squirt. Move it!" Patrick said to his younger sister, Emma. "I sit in the front, not you."

"I'm not moving," she said. "I was here first." Emma was twelve and closer in age to Luke than

Patrick was, but her brother still treated her like a child.

"Baby seats are in the back," Patrick said sarcastically.

"Stop it, you two. Just get in!" snapped Kate, Patrick's mother, as she jerked her thumb in the direction of the back seat of the van. Patrick and Luke clambered into the back.

"Your mom and dad called, Luke," said Kate. "They're going to be late. I said you could stay with us for supper. Is pizza OK with you?"

"Sure, thanks," said Luke.

She smiled at him and put the van in gear.

As they pulled away from the curb, Luke turned around and noticed the dark-green car pull slowly into the traffic behind them.

2

A Present for Patrick

*"Good evening. I'm Nathaniel
Benson with the ten o'clock news."*

"Come on, boys," Patrick's mother, Kate, called
from the kitchen. "Time to call it a night."

"Aw, come on, Mom," moaned Patrick. "It's not like there's school tomorrow."

"I realize summer vacation's just started," Kate replied, "but we have a big day tomorrow. There's your birthday party, and we have to finish packing to go to Grandma's on Sunday."

"This is a really awesome present," Luke said, looking at the watch Patrick had received for his birthday from his mother earlier that evening. It had a gold and silver band and looked very expensive. Luke was fascinated by the watch's face, which had Roman numerals on it. The watch had belonged to Patrick's dad, who died when Patrick was very young. It had six small dials around the edge depicting the time in Los Angeles, New York, London, Paris, Hong Kong and Tokyo. Luke turned it over in his hands, wondering if Patrick's dad had ever visited those cities.

"OK, you two. Time to get moving, Luke," Kate said. "I want to watch the rest of the news."

"... and in local news, industrialist Rupert Lennox died early this evening after a short illness. The

*founder and CEO of LennoxGen, Mr.
Lennox was a pioneer in genetic
research and test-tube-baby
technology. We'll have more on this
story after the break."*

Kate pressed the mute button and turned to
Luke. "Come on now, boys, before it gets too
dark."

"Okay," said Luke, standing up and heading
toward the front door. "Thanks for supper, Mrs.
Erickson."

"You're welcome, Luke," Kate called back.
"Oh, and Patrick, we're out of milk. Can you pick
up a carton at the convenience store before they
close?"

"No problem," Patrick said. "Hey, Luke, wait
up." Patrick joined Luke on the front porch. "We'd
better hurry," Patrick said, looking up at the
rapidly darkening sky, then glancing at his new
watch. "The store closes in five minutes."

"I'll race you there," said Luke. "Go!"

"Hey!" yelled Patrick, as Luke sprinted ahead.

Patrick gained on Luke as the two of them ran down the street, but Luke still reached the store first.

"Okay," Patrick gasped, after coming to a halt. "You win this time, but I'll beat you the next."

"You're just a sore loser," Luke said, grinning.

"See you at my party tomorrow," Patrick said, looking at his watch again.

"You bet," said Luke, waving to Patrick, who disappeared inside the convenience store.

As Luke hurried down the street, a dark-green car pulled up and parked across from the convenience store.

3
The Vanishing

Luke had overslept and was late for Patrick's party. He sprinted the last few blocks, turned the final corner and saw several police cars in front of Patrick's house.

A smartly dressed woman answered the door.

"Are you Luke Carpenter?" she asked.

"Yes."

"I'm Inspector Roberta Tremaine. Would you step into the kitchen, please?"

"What's happened?" Luke asked, glancing into the sitting-room.

A uniformed policewoman comforted Kate, who had her arm around Emma.

"We should leave Mrs. Erickson and Emma alone," whispered the inspector, stepping into the kitchen.

She gestured to Luke to sit down opposite her at the kitchen table. She was a middle-aged woman with a long thin face, high cheekbones and green eyes that reminded Luke of a cat. Her ash-blond hair was cut short, accentuating her slender neck.

"Patrick has run away from home. Do you have any idea where he might be, Luke?"

"What!"

"His mother said you were one of the last people to see him at the convenience store."

"I saw him go inside, but then I left."

"The store owner said Patrick bought some milk, but he never made it home."

"Are you sure he ran away?" Luke asked. "That's just not like him."

"That's why I wanted to talk to you. Can you think of anything Patrick said or did recently that might indicate he was planning something like this?"

"No, not at all. He was happy. It's his birthday today, and summer vacation is just starting. He was going to the coast tomorrow to stay with his grandparents. Have you checked with them?"

"Yes, we've talked to them, but they haven't seen or heard from him. We're doing everything we can to locate him, but we found this on the river bank."

She reached into her jacket pocket and pulled out a small plastic bag.

"His dad's watch!" Luke gasped.

"Was Patrick depressed about anything?"

"No, and he would never kill himself, if that's what you're asking."

"That's just one of the possibilities, but you need to be prepared to accept the worst."

Luke was stunned as the inspector handed him her business card.

"If you think of anything that might help our investigation, Luke, please give me a call."

As they left the kitchen, they saw Kate and Emma in the hallway.

"Thank you, Mrs. Erickson," said Inspector Tremaine, shaking Kate's hand. "I'll send someone over to check on you tomorrow. In the meantime, if you hear anything from Patrick, please call me immediately."

Kate nodded and gently pulled a sobbing Emma closer to her.

There was still no sign of Patrick three months later. It was mid-September, and school had resumed, as had Luke's after-school karate class. It had finished earlier than usual, so Luke stood outside the gym and waited for his father.

Grey clouds gathered overhead, and when the first few drops of rain fell, Luke took shelter under the canopy of a nearby office tower. A throng of men and women hurried out of the entrance and pushed past Luke on their way home from work. But one lone figure remained on the steps.

"Patrick?" asked Luke, stunned. But his friend didn't answer him. Luke reached over and grabbed his arm. "Patrick, where have you been?"

"Luke?" Patrick asked, offering a weak smile.

"Patrick, what happened to you?"

"Luke?" Patrick repeated, frowning at him. Then suddenly his expression changed. "Who are you?" he demanded angrily.

There was a look of fear in Patrick's eyes as he backed away from Luke toward the main entrance. "Get away from me!" he yelled.

The office tower doors suddenly swung open, and a large man with a shaved head hurried toward them. Right behind him was a tall thin man in a dark suit.

"Get the car, Merrick!" snapped Patrick. "And get this child out of my sight, Harriman!"

"At once, sir," said the tall thin man.

He gave a quick nod to his partner, then pulled a small radio from his jacket pocket, which was embroidered with the word LennoxGen. The taller man spoke into the radio as the bald man grabbed Luke tightly by the arm.

"Hey!" Luke shouted. "Let me go!"

"Shut up!" the bald man said, roughly pulling Luke into the rain. "You say anything about this to anyone and you're dead. Understand?"

The bald man didn't relax his grip until he had dragged Luke back to the entrance of the gym. By that time, a limousine with blacked-out windows had pulled up sharply at the curb. The bald man shoved Luke inside the gym and hurriedly joined the tall man and Patrick as they got into the limousine. Then it pulled away and disappeared into the rush hour traffic. Moments later, Luke's dad arrived.

"Sorry you had to wait in the rain, son, but the traffic was terrible."

Still stunned, Luke got into the car.

"That's OK, Dad," he said.

He considered mentioning the incident, but the memory of the bald man's words stopped him.

As soon as Luke got inside the house, he ran up to his room, turned on his computer and typed LennoxGen into the search engine.

LennoxGen had been founded twenty years earlier by billionaire industrialist Rupert Lennox. Luke clicked on a link and found a picture of Lennox taken when the government began hearings on stem cell research. LennoxGen had been a pioneer in infertility treatment but was now focused on genetic research.

Ten minutes later Luke stood on the Ericksons' front porch. He swallowed hard and pressed the doorbell. Emma opened the door.

"Hi, Luke. Mom's just at the store, but you can wait if you want. She won't be long."

"Thanks," Luke said, following Emma into the living room.

She curled up in an armchair and turned the TV on while Luke sat opposite her on the sofa.

"Actually," Luke said, "I came to see you."

"Really?"

"Yes," said Luke, turning the TV off. "I know this may sound weird, but I think I saw Patrick a few hours ago."

"What! Where?"

"Downtown."

"Are you sure?"

"Pretty sure. He seemed to recognize me at first, but he suddenly got angry and started yelling at me. Then a guy from LennoxGen pulled me away and threatened to kill me if I told anyone anything about what had happened."

"What's LennoxGen?"

"A drug company."

Just then, the front door opened.

"Emma?" her mother called out from the hallway.

"Don't tell your mother or anyone else anything about this," Luke whispered urgently. "Meet me at the tennis courts in an hour."

"Oh, hi, Luke," Kate said, entering the living room. "What brings you here?"

"Just checking in, Mrs. Erickson."

"It's very nice of you to stop by, Luke. Would you like to stay for dinner?"

"Sorry, but I have to run. I told Mom I'd be right home. But thanks for the invitation."

"Okay. Stop in anytime, Luke. It's always a pleasure to see you."

"Goodbye, Mrs. Erickson. Goodbye, Emma."

"See you later, Luke," Emma said, with a quick nod.

An hour later, Luke met Emma at the tennis courts near the community centre.

"I never really bought the idea that Patrick ran away or committed suicide," said Emma.

"Me neither. It never added up, despite what the police told us."

"I checked out LennoxGen on the Web too. If we want answers, we have to go there."

"But what if they recognize me?"

"You saw Patrick at their downtown office. We'll go to their research facility just outside of town."

"They won't let kids into a place like that. We'll never get access."

"We'll tell them we're reporters for the school newspaper. We've got a couple of professional days off school, so we can try tomorrow."

"OK, but will LennoxGen go for it?"

"They already have," said Emma, with a smile. "We have an appointment at nine-thirty."

4 LennoxGen

The LennoxGen research facility was a sprawling concrete and glass three-storey complex located in an industrial park close to the airport. The entire facility was surrounded by a wire fence with a security booth at the gates. Emerald lawns and neatly trimmed shrubs framed the complex.

At the security booth, Luke explained to the guard that he and Emma were there to meet with Lisa MacKenzie in the public relations department. The guard made a quick call to reception, then waved them in.

Suspended over the entrance was a huge chrome globe with black letters spelling *LennoxGen*. As Luke and Emma walked beneath it, double glass doors automatically opened, and they found themselves in the reception area.

"LennoxGen. Can you hold, please?" A middle-aged woman seated at the reception desk put down the phone and looked at them. "Good morning. May I help you?"

"We have an appointment with Lisa MacKenzie," Emma said. "We're from the Abbeyglenn School Times."

"Please take a seat while I call her."

Luke and Emma sat down on a sofa opposite the reception desk. The coffee table in front of them was littered with magazines devoted to current affairs, and medical and scientific topics. Luke was about to select one when the glass doors opposite him slid open. A young woman with shoulder-length blond hair and dressed in a smart navy-blue business suit entered the reception area.

"Hello," she said extending her hand. "You must be Emma and Luke from Abbeyglenn School. I'm Lisa MacKenzie. I've made an appointment for you with Dr. William Pender, our director of research. He's normally very busy, so you're very lucky to get the chance to ask him some questions. Shall we get started?"

They both nodded, and Lisa ushered them over to the glass doors. She took a slim plastic card from her jacket pocket and slid it down the slot on the wall. The doors parted and they stepped through.

"Does that card give you access to the entire complex?" Emma asked.

"No," replied Lisa. "There are high security areas that require special cards."

Lisa led the way through a maze of corridors, past large rooms filled with computers and scientific and medical equipment. They passed

LennoxGen staff dressed in white lab coats or business attire. The entire complex was a hive of activity. They walked past a lunchroom filled with dining tables, sofas and armchairs.

"That's the employee lounge," Lisa told them.

Luke glanced in and recognized the two men he had seen outside the downtown LennoxGen office. He quickly turned his head away so they wouldn't see him.

Lisa continued along the hallway and stopped in front of a door that had *Director of Research* inlaid into the wood in bold black letters. She was about to knock on the door when it suddenly swung open, revealing a thin man with a long face and grey hair.

"Hello, Dr. Simpson," said Lisa.

He looked disdainfully at her and went on his way without a word.

Inside the office, one wall was covered in certificates, diplomas, expensive-looking artwork and shelves filled with sculptures and framed photographs. The opposite wall was taken up completely by a well-stocked bookcase, crammed with scientific volumes. On one corner of the wide polished desk was a fierce Aztec stone figure. A man stood behind the desk with his back to them, gazing through the window at the extensive lawns that surrounded the LennoxGen facility.

"Emma, Luke," said Lisa. "This is Dr. William Pender, our director of research."

The figure at the window turned around. Dr. Pender was a tall well-dressed man with dark wavy hair and a thick moustache.

"I'm afraid I'm extremely busy this morning, Miss MacKenzie."

"I know, Dr. Pender," Lisa apologized, "but this shouldn't take long. Can you please give them a few minutes of your time? They want to interview you for their school newspaper."

"Very well," said Pender gruffly.

"Thanks, Doctor," Lisa said. "I'll be back shortly."

"Well," said Dr. Pender once Lisa had left, "what would you like to know?"

"Could you give us a brief history of your association with LennoxGen?" Emma asked, taking out her notebook.

"I originally founded a company that specialized in brain and memory research. As the recognized expert in the field, I attracted Mr. Lennox's attention, and he offered me the directorship of his rescarch facility."

"Doctor Pender," said a voice over the intercom on his desk, "the president has left his office again."

"Alert security," Pender ordered into the intercom. "He can't have gone far."

Then he turned to Luke and Emma.

"My apologies," he said, ushering them out of his office. "Wait right here, please. I'll have Miss MacKenzie meet you in a few moments."

"Okay. Thanks you for your time," Luke said.

Dr. Pender closed his office door and headed off down the corridor. The moment he rounded the corner, Luke grabbed Emma's arm.

"Come on! Let's follow him," whispered Luke. "Maybe we can get some clues about what happened to Patrick."

Luke and Emma followed him at a distance. But as they approached the lunchroom, a crowd of LennoxGen staff poured out of their offices into the hallway, headed for their coffee break. Hoping to spot Dr. Pender, Luke and Emma joined the group streaming into the lunchroom.

When they reached the entrance, they saw Patrick working on a laptop computer at one of the tables.

5
The Child Inside

Emma stared open-mouthed at her lost brother. She was about to dart across the room when Luke stopped her.

"Act casual. We don't want to attract any attention."

Emma nodded as Luke scanned the room. The staff were engaged in conversation, laughing and joking as they filled their trays. Luke noticed Dr. Simpson chatting to an older woman in a white lab coat at a table against the far wall. Patrick sat alone at a round table in the centre of the room, and Luke and Emma slowly walked toward him.

"Patrick," Emma faltered.

Patrick looked up and stared at Luke and Emma.

"Emma? Luke?" he muttered, flashing a brief smile of recognition.

"What's going on?" asked Emma, cautiously touching her brother's arm.

Suddenly Patrick's expression changed. He stood up from the table and began to back away.

"What are you kids doing here?" he demanded. "Security! Security!"

"What's wrong with you?" Emma asked.

"Nothing at all," Patrick said. "Security! Security! Get these kids out of here."

"You two?" growled a voice behind Luke. "I told you to wait outside my office."

It was Pender, accompanied by the two men Luke had encountered outside the downtown office tower.

Pender turned and spoke to Patrick: "We should go back to your office, sir." He then signalled to Harriman. "Lock these kids up, and meet me in Mr. Lennox's office."

Harriman grabbed Luke and Emma by the arms and began to escort them out of the lunchroom.

"No need to be alarmed. Everything is under control," Merrick reassured the staff.

"You can't do this!" Emma cried, as Harriman pulled her and Luke into the hallway.

But Harriman said nothing. When they reached his office, he dragged Luke and Emma inside.

"I warned you downtown what would happen," Harriman snarled, as he left the office and locked the door behind him.

"We've got to find a way out of here, fast," Luke said.

"Someone's coming," Emma said, and the door swung open. It was Lisa MacKenzie.

"Quick, come with me," Lisa said.

Emma and Luke followed her into the corridor and down the nearest stairwell. They entered the underground parking and headed for a car.

"Get in the back, and lie down flat," Lisa told them, as she unlocked the doors.

Once Luke and Emma were safely hidden, Lisa drove out of the complex.

"We're safe now," Lisa said. "You can sit up. But I've only got a few minutes before they connect me with your disappearance. So I'll have to drop you at a bus stop and get back as quickly as possible."

"Why are you helping us?" Emma asked.

"There have been all sorts of rumours ever since that boy appeared at LennoxGen. The most persistent is that he's a relative of the late Mr. Lennox, and he's being groomed to take over the company when he's old enough."

"That's not true," said Luke.

"He's my brother, Patrick," Emma added.

"And my best friend," continued Luke. "He suddenly disappeared at the start of the summer holidays."

"The police thought he was a runaway or a suicide, but Patrick would never do that," Emma said.

Then Luke told Lisa what had happened outside the office tower.

"Patrick recognized you there?" Lisa asked.

"Yes," said Luke, "but then Merrick arrived and Harriman grabbed me. Before I could get near Patrick again, he was pushed into a limousine and driven away."

"I have an idea what's going on," Lisa said, "but I'll have to do more digging around and see what else I can come up with. In the meantime, don't say anything until you hear from me. And don't trust anyone."

She stopped the car at the bus stop.

"Here's my card," she said, handing it to Emma. "Be careful. Your lives are in danger."

Emma and Luke got out and Lisa sped off back to LennoxGen.

6
The List

"Luke, wake up. There's a phone call for you," his mother said, opening the door to his room.

Luke hurried downstairs and picked up the phone. It was Emma.

"I just tried to reach Lisa at LennoxGen, but they said she doesn't work there any more."

"What happened?"

"The receptionist wouldn't give me any information, but Lisa sent us something. You should get over here right away. But come through the alley. There's a dark-green van that's been parked across from our house for most of the morning."

Fifteen minutes later, Luke slipped through the back door into the Ericksons' kitchen.

"Is the van still parked out front?" Luke asked.

"Yes," Emma answered.

"Is this what Lisa sent us?" he asked, picking up the envelope on the table. "Has your mom seen it?"

"No, she wasn't here when the courier came. What about your parents?"

"I haven't told them a thing."

Emma emptied the contents of the envelope onto the table.

"There's a plastic card, an old press release, a note and this," Emma said, handing Luke a computer disc.

"What's on it?"

"I don't know. It keeps asking for a password, and I haven't been able to figure it out. I thought you might have more luck, but you should read this first."

She pushed the note over to Luke.

> *Luke and Emma,*
>
> *Open the disc, make a copy of it, and get in touch with me immediately.*
>
> *Lisa*

"What's on the other paper?" Luke asked as he reached for it.

"It's all about Pender."

Luke scanned the details. It was a press release dated from several years earlier when Pender had first joined LennoxGen. It described his research with patients suffering from multiple personality disorder.

Emma picked up the plastic card and turned it over. It had a number on the back.

"I think this is one of those swipe cards they use to open the security doors at LennoxGen," she said.

"Let's try and open the disc. Maybe it will explain all of this."

They went up to Emma's room, and Luke sat down at the computer. He inserted the disc into the drive. After the LennoxGen logo dissolved, a box appeared asking for a password.

"I tried everything I could think of," said Emma.

"Maybe it's a series of numbers instead of a word. Let's try the number on the back of the swipe card."

He typed in *B6270*.

Access granted immediately appeared in the centre of the screen. On a sidebar were three buttons, entitled *Locations*, *Personnel* and *Subscribers*. Luke clicked on *Locations*, and the screen changed to show a map of the world speckled with numerous red dots.

"Let's look at North America," Emma suggested.

With a click of the mouse, the map disappeared and was replaced by a list of medical clinics scattered across the continent.

"These might be branch offices for the company's genetic research," said Emma.

"I don't think so. This one's devoted to infertility treatment, and so is this one." Luke scrolled down the list. "In fact all of them are."

"Click on *Personnel*."

Luke clicked on *Personnel* and opened up a long list of medical doctors. Beneath the names were the doctors' areas of expertise, along with a list of the institutions where they had done most of their work over the years. They were all experts in infertility treatment.

"This is very odd," said Luke.

"Why? Isn't LennoxGen one of the world's leaders in this sort of thing?"

"They started off in that field and still have an interest in it," said Luke. "But it's all about genetics there now. Let's check the *Subscribers* section."

A new page opened, with three columns. One was entitled *Subscribers*, and the second was headed *Suppliers*. A third column, entitled *Status*, was empty. However, the first two columns contained long lists of names and addresses from all over the world. Luke scrolled down the list until he reached two names at the end. Both were highlighted in red.

"Cornelius Zenden and Marina Kohler," said Emma. "Wonder who they are?"

"Zenden is the CEO of SoftScience Corporation," Luke said after clicking on the name. "He lives in Seattle."

"Go back and see who Kohler is."

"Marina Kohler is the director of the Zurich Institute of International Finance."

"Click on the icon above her name that looks like a padlock," Emma suggested.

"Okay."

A page appeared with the word *Picasso* opposite a picture of Emma with her name written underneath it.

Emma and Luke both gasped.

Luke quickly clicked on the padlock above Zenden's name. A page opened that had a picture of Luke with his name underneath it and the word *aurora* opposite.

"This is creepy, Luke. Maybe we should tell our parents."

"What? That our names are on some list and we think we've seen your brother?"

"Okay, then let's take the disc to the police."

"They won't listen to us."

"Inspector Tremaine will," Emma said, looking out the window. "She's kept in touch with us. She'll know what to do about all of this, but let's go out the back. That van is still parked outside, and there's no sense taking any chances."

Inspector Tremaine

The local police station was a low-rise building constructed from dull grey concrete. A colourful shield with the city's coat of arms was inlaid into the masonry above the front entrance, which had tall thick shrubs on either side.

As Emma went through the double doors, Luke turned and saw the dark van pull up and park across street.

"We're here to see Inspector Tremaine," Emma told the desk sergeant.

"I'll call her. Who should I say is here?"

"Emma Erickson and Luke Carpenter."

"Just a moment," said the sergeant.

He picked up the phone on the front desk, punched in a couple of numbers and spoke with the inspector. In a few moments, Inspector Tremaine appeared and led Luke and Emma to her office.

"So," Tremaine asked, offering them a seat opposite her desk, "do you have any new leads?"

"We saw Patrick," Luke said.

"Where?" Tremaine asked.

"I saw him outside the LennoxGen downtown office tower," Luke said, "a couple of days ago."

"And then we saw him yesterday at their research facility," Emma added.

"LennoxGen?" asked Tremaine. "I think you're probably mistaken. What would Patrick be doing there? And how did you get in?"

"We pretended to be reporters for our school newspaper," Emma explained.

Then Luke handed the inspector the computer disc.

"Where did you get this?" Tremaine asked, turning it over in her hand.

"From Lisa MacKenzie, at the LennoxGen public relations department," Emma said. "She sent it to me today."

"And it has photos of us on it opposite the names of two people, Cornelius Zenden and Marina Kohler," Luke added.

"Very interesting," Tremaine said, slipping the disc into her pocket. "I'll have one of our computer experts take a look at this. Wait here. I'll be right back," she said, leaving the office.

Luke got up and went to the window to see if the dark-green van was still there.

"What are you looking at?" Emma asked.

"The green van is out there."

As he turned back toward Emma, Luke saw the email screen on Inspector Tremaine's computer. A new email had suddenly appeared with the subject line *Urgent – Zenden & Kohler dead*.

Luke grabbed the mouse and quickly opened the email.

"What are you doing?" Emma asked.

"Come over here and take a look at this."

From: Pender, William

Subject: Urgent – Zenden & Kohler Dead

Tremaine: Zenden and Kohler killed in car accident in Switzerland. Subjects must be made ready for pick-up and delivery.

"We have to get out of here now!" Luke whispered.

"What about the disc? We forgot to copy it," Emma said under her breath.

"No time to worry about that. Let's go!"

They quickly slipped out of the office, past the sergeant at the front desk and through the front door. They were about to make a run for it when a car raced into the parking lot. Luke and Emma scurried behind the shrubs beside the entrance as the car screeched to a halt. They watched Harriman leap out of the car, followed by two other men. The instant the men disappeared inside the station, Luke and Emma sprinted across the street and into the nearest alley.

Journey into Jeopardy

From their hiding place, Luke and Emma could see the front of the police station. Harriman emerged into the parking lot and began barking orders on his cellphone. After the other two men joined him, Harriman snapped his phone shut. Then all three men got back into the car and drove off.

"What now?" Emma asked.

"We have to go back to LennoxGen."

"Are you crazy?"

"Well, what do you suggest?"

"Let's tell our parents."

"They won't believe us. We have to handle this on our own. Look." Luke reached into his pocket and pulled out the swipe card. "Lisa sent us this, and the number on it opened the disc. It might also open the security doors where they're keeping Patrick."

"OK," Emma reluctantly agreed.

They emerged from the alleyway next to a bus stop outside a drugstore. Luke and Emma darted inside just as a police car cruised by, followed by the van and the LennoxGen car. As soon as they passed, a bus pulled up, and Luke and Emma quickly boarded it. Twenty minutes later, they got off and walked the last few blocks to the LennoxGen research facility.

As they approached the main gate, Luke stopped and pointed to the security guard.

"He's checking identities," Luke said. "We'll never get in."

"What about those construction trucks coming out of that other gate? The security guard's letting them drive through. We could hop in the back of one of the trucks."

There were four trucks lined up along the sidewalk. Their engines idled while the drivers waited to be waved through security. Luke and Emma hurried over to the back of the fourth truck.

Emma climbed into the truck and Luke quickly followed, tumbling headfirst into the back as the truck slowly rolled forward. He landed with a thud on a pile of bricks, rolls of electrical cable and other building materials.

"What kept you?" asked Emma, with a smirk.

The truck came to a sudden halt, then moved through the security checkpoint. A few moments later the truck backed into a loading dock at the rear of the complex.

"Let's go," said Luke.

Luke and Emma jumped out and hid behind a collection of wooden pallets as a group of construction workers passed by. Then they used Lisa's security card to enter the rear of the main building.

"Which way now?" Luke asked.

"Let's try the right corridor."

The hallway was deserted. They didn't run into any LennoxGen employees until they turned a corner, where they almost collided with a tall man. He had a thick mop of brown hair and was carrying a clipboard.

"Hello," he said warmly, peering at them over his glasses. "What are you kids doing here?"

"It's kids' day," Emma said quickly. "Our mom works here, and they said she could invite me and my brother in today."

"Really?" said the man, frowning. "I must have missed the memo."

"My mother's office is right here," Emma declared, pointing to a door. "She gave us her swipe card and told us to wait inside for her."

Luke looked over and saw *B6270* written on the door. Emma inserted the card into a slot, and the door unlocked with a short buzzing sound.

"Thanks," she said, waving to the man and pulling Luke inside the office. The room was filled with computer terminals and filing cabinets.

"Let's try the computer," Emma said, sitting down at the nearest desk.

Luke pulled up a chair beside her and watched as she used the same password to open up a series of files.

"Try that one," Luke suggested, pointing to a heading that read *International Operations*.

Emma clicked on the icon, and together they read the information on the screen.

> *LennoxGen in Zurich is responsible for European operations and is under the direction of Dr. Josef Muller.*

"Someone's coming," whispered Emma.

Before the door opened, Luke and Emma slipped out of sight under one of the desks.

9
The Lethal Laboratory

Luke and Emma watched as Dr. Simpson came into the room. He headed for a filing cabinet set against the opposite wall, opened the top drawer and pulled out an assortment of files. As he closed the drawer, Pender entered the room.

"Ah, Simpson," he said. "I was looking for you. Have you downloaded the Kohler brain scan from Zurich yet?"

"Yes, it came through an hour ago. I was just getting Zenden's file. Everything will be ready once Tremaine delivers Emma and Luke. What's their status?"

"They managed to slip away from her, but it's only a matter of time before we catch them."

"How are things going with Mr. Lennox? Have you been able to stabilize him yet?"

"The boy's personality still asserts itself every now and then, but the new medication is taking effect and is more successful at suppressing it. A few more doses and the process should be permanent."

"Doctor Pender, the president is asking for you," the intercom announced.

"I have to go," Pender said, "but I'll let you know as soon as we secure the girl."

"Fine, I'll be in my lab."

As soon as the doctors left the room, Luke and Emma emerged from their hiding place.

"They're going to use our bodies for some kind of brain transplant," Luke said. "Let's get out of here fast!"

"But we came here to rescue Patrick."

"How do we do that? We have no idea where they're keeping him."

"I know, but we have to try."

"OK, let's go."

Luke cautiously opened the door and spotted Simpson stepping into an elevator.

"Let's follow Simpson," Luke said, stepping into the corridor.

They quickly headed over to the elevator.

"There's only one button," Emma said, when they got inside. She pushed it, but the doors opened again.

"Try Lisa's pass," said Luke.

Emma took the swipe card from her pocket and inserted it into the slot on the panel. As she slid it to the left, a tiny light changed from red to green, and the doors closed. The elevator descended rapidly. It came to a halt and the doors slid open. Luke and Emma quickly stepped out into a deserted passageway, where they heard the low hum of machinery.

They made their way cautiously along a corridor but walked right into Merrick as they rounded the first corner.

"Well, look who we have here!" Merrick said, reaching out to grab them.

Luke and Emma turned and ran in the opposite direction, but landed right in Harriman's arms.

"Seems you've saved us a lot of trouble," Harriman said, securing Luke's arm in a vice-like grip.

Merrick came up behind Emma and grabbed her by the wrist.

"I'll take the girl to Simpson's lab in section eighteen," Merrick said. "You take the boy to Lennox."

10
The Madness of Rupert Lennox

Luke's heart pounded as Harriman dragged him through the underground complex. Finally they reached a pair of ornate oak doors, and Harriman knocked.

"Come in," a voice said.

Harriman opened the doors and pulled Luke inside a huge room. There were several tall bookshelves and a large aquarium against one wall. A collection of paintings and shelves filled with sculptures adorned another one. Patrick, seated behind a desk, was engaged in a telephone conversation. Behind him, floor-to-ceiling monitors showed scenes from the entire LennoxGen complex. Dr. Pender, who had been observing the monitors, signalled Harriman to bring Luke over to the desk.

"Has the girl been secured?" Pender asked.

"Merrick took her directly to Simpson's lab," Harriman assured him.

"Good."

"Luke, isn't it?" Patrick said, after hanging up the phone. "Take a seat, young man."

Luke sat on a chair in front of the desk.

"You've been very clever," Patrick said, "you and your little friend. But this is as far as you go. In a few hours you and the girl will be history."

The phone on the desk rang.

"Rupert Lennox," Patrick said, answering it. "Excellent. Keep me informed." He turned to Pender. "Simpson has begun the download procedure."

Luke shivered.

"It's wonderful to be alive again, thanks to your friend," Patrick grinned. "He was my clone, and now his body is mine."

"This will never work!" Luke shouted.

"It is working, and your time is over," said Pender.

"Take him to your lab and download Zenden," Patrick said. Harriman grabbed Luke's arms.

"I'll send Harriman back with the final dose of your medication," Pender said. "Make sure you take it right away."

"Very well," Patrick said as they left the office.

"Don't worry; it's completely painless," Pender said to Luke. "I developed this procedure several years ago. That was when I first discovered a way to download a person's memory from their brain with minimal side effects."

As they reached the elevator doors, Harriman pressed the down button while Pender continued talking.

"At the same time, LennoxGen had been secretly working on human cloning and had achieved stunning results. When we combined their research with my memory download procedure, we were able to achieve a form of immortality."

"Was Patrick the first?" asked Luke, as they entered the elevator.

"No, he wasn't," Pender answered. "Mr. Lennox's health failed unexpectedly, so we had to secure his clone earlier than anticipated. We knew the procedure would work. We had already created a clone of industrialist Alexander Frederickson and used one of LennoxGen's infertility clinics to implant it into an unsuspecting woman. When the boy turned fifteen, we downloaded Frederickson's memory into him and achieved our first success. Since that time, Alexander Frederickson has continued running his global enterprises from a secret European location."

As they left the elevator, Pender continued.

"We then decided to offer the same service to others, for a price. We're tracking over seventy-five clones of some of the world's wealthiest and most powerful people. We've downloaded their memories, and we update them monthly in case of a sudden death. Once Patrick's body has aged sufficiently, he will be presented to the world as Mr. Lennox's long-lost grandson and will inherit the company."

"So my parents aren't my real parents?" Luke asked.

"No, they aren't," said Pender. "You don't really have genetic parents."

"You're a liar!" Luke screamed back at him.

They turned a corner and stopped in front of Pender's laboratory. He slid his card down the slot while Harriman kept a tight grip on Luke.

"You'll never get away with this," Luke said.

"Ah, but we already have," Pender said with a smirk, opening the door to the lab and ushering Luke inside. "By this evening you and the girl will have been officially declared dead according to police reports."

"You can't keep this project a secret forever," Luke said, defiantly. "One of your employees is bound to let something slip."

"Perhaps," mused Pender, "but we have, shall we call it, an insurance policy. Our key employees all over the globe also have clones. They too share in the promise of eternal life, as long as they keep their mouths shut. They have plenty to lose if they don't remain loyal."

"What about Lisa MacKenzie?" Luke asked.

"Miss MacKenzie's snooping almost ruined decades of secret work, but she'll soon be disposed of," Pender said.

11
Erased

Banks of computers ran the length of one wall inside Pender's lab. The stainless-steel room had a strong antiseptic smell that emanated from a small table filled with surgical instruments. In the centre of the ceiling hung two mechanical arms that reminded Luke of the drills in a dentist's office. A long narrow table underneath them was equipped with wrist and ankle restraints.

"Strap the boy down," Pender ordered.

Luke aimed a kick at Harriman, but the big man blocked it, lifted Luke onto the table and strapped him down.

"Now, be a good boy," Pender said, grabbing a nearby syringe. "I don't want to have to inject you with this. There's enough sedative in here to floor a charging bull elephant."

Once Luke was secured, Pender put the syringe down on a nearby table. Then the telephone rang, and Pender answered it.

"No need to worry, Tremaine. We have both of them," Pender said. He put down the phone and turned to Luke. "It's so useful to have a member of the law on our payroll. Wouldn't you agree, Harriman?"

"Absolutely. When someone has to disappear, there can be awkward questions. But Tremaine makes it look like an ordinary missing person case, unsolved of course."

Pender handed Harriman a bottle of pills. "Deliver these to Mr. Lennox, and make sure he takes them."

As soon as Harriman left, Pender turned back to Luke. "Enjoy your last few minutes as Luke Carpenter," he sneered.

Pender attached a number of electrodes to Luke's head and placed a blindfold over his eyes. Luke heard the click of a switch, and suddenly a flood of unfamiliar images flashed through his mind. It was over in seconds, but Luke was surprised to find his own mind still intact.

"Mr. Zenden, wake up," Pender said.

The blindfold was removed, and Luke saw Pender looming over him.

"What is the password?" Pender asked.

At first, Luke wasn't sure what to say, but then he remembered the word next to his name in Zenden's computer file.

"Aurora," Luke answered.

"Excellent! The download was a success," Pender said, unstrapping him. "Welcome to LennoxGen, Mr. Zenden."

He helped Luke sit up on the table and handed him a glass of water and a pill.

"It's better if you rest and gather your strength. You'll have to take one of these twice a day for the next couple of weeks."

The telephone rang again, and when Pender turned to pick it up Luke quickly drank the water and shoved the pill into his pocket. Then he grabbed the syringe, hid it under his leg, closed his eyes and lay back down.

"Pender here...Ah, Simpson. How did the Kohler download go?...Hmm, have you tried the back-up yet?...Yes, the download here was a success. Zenden's resting after his first dose of medication. Let me know what happens with the back-up," he said, hanging up the phone.

Suddenly, the door opened and Merrick rushed in.

"Harriman needs your help with Mr. Lennox, doctor."

"Stay here with Mr. Zenden," Pender said, looking over at the empty glass. "I'm not sure how long he'll sleep, but someone should be here when he wakes up. After that, Simpson can take over. He hasn't seen Mr. Zenden since the Vienna conference. They'll have a lot of catching up to do. I'll be back as soon as I can. What have you done with MacKenzie?"

"I've got her strapped down in 226."

"Good. You can dispose of her when I get back," Pender said, handing him a sheet of paper. "Here are some facts about Zenden. If he wakes up, read them to him. It'll help reorient him."

After Pender left the room, Merrick walked over to Luke. Instantly, Luke plunged the syringe into Merrick's thigh.

"What!" Merrick gasped, and slumped to the floor.

Luke leapt off the table, quickly searched Merrick's pockets and grabbed his pass card. Then he picked up the sheet of paper lying on the floor next to Merrick and quickly scanned the details of Zenden's life. Luke stuffed it into his pocket and stepped cautiously out into the corridor. In a few moments he located room 226. Merrick's card released the lock, and Luke saw Lisa, gagged and strapped down on a metal table.

12
Changing Minds

"Luke!" Lisa exclaimed after he released her. "Where's Emma?"

"Simpson's got her and has started the download procedure. It's like a horrible nightmare. Pender just tried to download Zenden into me, but for some reason the procedure didn't work."

"So they *are* still having trouble perfecting the transfer. Does Pender know it didn't work?"

"No. I was able to remember the password on the disc, and that convinced him the download was a success."

"Does Emma know the Kohler password?"

"She saw it opposite her name, but she might not remember."

"We'd better move fast. Do you know where she is?"

"Harriman mentioned section eighteen."

"Follow me," said Lisa, as she grabbed a lab coat from a hook behind the door. "If anyone asks any questions, I'll tell them I'm escorting you to the lab for your download procedure."

As the two of them headed down the hallway, Luke told her about Tremaine.

"This is much worse than I thought. There's a copy of all the research reports on a disc hidden in my office. We'll need it for evidence if we're going to blow the lid on LennoxGen."

"Do you think there's a way for us to save Patrick? They're still having problems with

Lennox's memory, but they're treating him with medication."

"I don't know," Lisa said, "but this is section eighteen."

Lisa and Luke emerged from the hallway into an open, circular foyer. Two steel spiral staircases rose up to a narrow observation area directly above them.

"This way," Lisa said softly, heading up the nearest set of steps.

Luke followed her to the top, and they peered over a railing into the lab. Banks of monitors lined one wall, and in front of one of them stood Simpson. Behind him, strapped to a steel table, lay Emma, partially covered by a white sheet. A number of electrodes were fastened to her forehead and connected to a nearby computer.

"Is the back-up procedure working?" asked a woman in a lab coat, entering the room.

"There's been an unexpected slowdown, Dr. Nelson. The girl's personality is fighting back."

"Fascinating—like the body's natural defences attacking a virus."

"Yes. Keep an eye on the girl's brainwave patterns."

Dr. Nelson went over to check the computer monitors closest to Emma.

Lisa signalled for Luke to follow her back down the spiral staircase. Then she led him into a nearby chemical storage room. There were shelves filled with bottles and vials containing fluids and powders with warning labels. A long steel table stood next to a sink flanked by cabinets and cupboards.

"There must be something here we can use," Lisa said, quickly scanning the shelves on both sides of the room. "Aha," she said, reaching for a bottle filled with a pale pink liquid. "This should do nicely."

"What is it?"

"No idea, but look at the label: *Highly Flammable*. This should set off the fire alarms," Lisa said, pulling a blue lighter from the pocket of the lab coat.

She uncorked the bottle and poured the liquid onto the table. Then she walked over to the sink and pulled a couple of paper towels from the dispenser on the wall.

"Better not get too close," she cautioned, lighting the towels.

She held them at arm's length, dropped the flaming paper onto the table and quickly backed away. The pool of liquid burst into flame and shot into the air in all directions. Glass popped and cracked as bottles and vials exploded. In seconds, half of the room was an inferno.

"Was that supposed to happen?" Luke asked nervously.

Lisa grabbed Luke's arm and pulled him back up the stairs above the foyer just as the fire alarms went off. Dr. Nelson and Dr. Simpson rushed out of the lab.

"Come on!" shouted Luke. "Let's get Emma before he comes back!"

The fire burst through the wall into the lab, and the sprinklers couldn't contain the flames. Luke and Lisa hurried over to Emma and ripped the wires from her head. As Luke unstrapped her and eased her off the table, Emma's eyes flickered open.

"Emma," said Luke. "Emma, do you know who I am?"

"Luke?"

"Yes. Can you walk on your own?"

"I think so."

"This way," Lisa shouted as she ran back into the foyer.

LennoxGen workers ran past them toward the stairway.

"We have to find Patrick!" Emma shouted.

"I know where he is," Luke hollered. "He's in an office one level up."

"I have to get the disc from my office before the fire spreads," said Lisa. "Can you two find Patrick without me?"

"Yes," Luke yelled back. "We'll meet up with you outside later."

"The elevators will be out of action. We'll have to use the stairway. If the smoke gets too thick, be sure to crouch down and keep moving," Lisa shouted to them.

They followed Lisa up the stairway. The fire hadn't spread there yet. Luke and Emma exited on the next level.

When they arrived at Lennox's office, the double doors were wide open, and the room was empty. The security monitors on the far wall showed the fire rapidly raging out of control as LennoxGen's employees streamed out of the building.

"They must have taken Patrick to a safer location," Luke said, approaching the desk. "But they left his medication." He grabbed a small brown plastic bottle near the phone.

"Where do you think they would've taken him?"

"I don't know, but we should get out of here before the fire spreads up here."

As they turned to leave, the first hint of smoke started to pour through the vents. But Dr. Pender stood at the door and blocked their way.

"Where's Patrick?" Luke demanded.

"Mr. Lennox is in a safe place," Pender sneered. "Give me that bottle, and I'll let you leave."

"No way," Luke said. "It's all over for you and LennoxGen."

As Pender advanced menacingly toward Luke, he backed up to the aquarium.

"Come one step closer," Luke threatened, holding up the bottle, "and I'll feed this to the fish."

Pender lunged for Luke, who dropped the bottle into the water.

"You fool!" Pender screamed in a rage.

He picked up a paperweight from the desk and smashed the glass of the aquarium. Water and priceless tropical fish poured out all over the carpet. Pender slipped, fell backwards and cut his hands on the shattered glass. As he tried to grab the medicine, the wall of monitors exploded in flames.

"Run!" Emma yelled.

As Luke and Emma rushed through the doorway, a huge fireball ripped across the office. Fire alarms blared and echoed through the hallways. Water rained down from the sprinklers. Luke and Emma raced up the stairs.

"We can't go any farther!" Luke yelled. "There's a huge wall of smoke coming up the stairs."

"Lisa said to crouch and keep moving."

Luke and Emma got down on their knees and crawled forward, but the heat was so intense that the stairs below them suddenly collapsed.

"We have to get out now!" Luke screamed and plunged through the nearest door with Emma right behind him.

"This is the main floor!" Emma yelled. "There's an exit sign. Follow me."

As they turned the corner, an explosion rocked the corridor and knocked them both down. Scrambling to his feet, Luke spun around and saw Emma still lying on the ground. Suddenly, fire crews rushed past him, lifted her onto a stretcher and carried her outside. Luke followed closely behind.

It was dusk now, and the front lawns were filled with fire trucks, police cars and ambulances. Paramedics and police officers treated LennoxGen employees who were hurt or overcome by smoke inhalation.

The firemen took Emma to a waiting ambulance while a paramedic checked Luke's condition. After a few quick questions, they released him.

A TV crew had arrived to cover the blaze. In the centre of one of the lawns, with the smoking LennoxGen facility behind him, Nathaniel Benson stood recording a segment for the evening news. Next to him, Simpson was talking to a police officer.

Luke went over to check on Emma, who had been placed inside an ambulance.

"The paramedics say you're going to be OK," he assured her. "Just an overnight stay in the hospital."

"What should I tell the police if they ask me any questions?"

"Just stick with that story about being here for the school newspaper. They should believe that."

"What about Patrick?"

"Don't worry. I have an idea."

13
Masquerade

After Luke watched the ambulance drive away, he looked around for Lisa but didn't see her anywhere. Then he saw Simpson talking to the LennoxGen employees as they waited on the lawns for medical attention. When Simpson walked away from the others, Luke swallowed hard and approached him.

"Doctor Simpson," said Luke. "I haven't seen you since the Vienna conference."

Simpson turned around and looked curiously at him.

"Mr. Zenden?" he asked hesitantly.

"Yes," said Luke.

"Remarkable," said Simpson, studying Luke's face. "I didn't work directly on the Lennox transfer, but we've had some problems with the results. Pender told me he'd made some modifications, but this is beyond my expectations. Do you know what happened to him?"

"No, he wasn't in the room when the alarm went off."

"I've been asking around and no one has seen him. I don't think he made it out."

"What about Lennox?" Luke asked.

"Harriman took him to the LennoxGen private airport. We have a plane waiting to fly you to Zurich along with Lennox and Marina, but it doesn't look like she made it out."

"Marina?"

"You were both killed in a car accident. I was just downloading Marina's memory file into her clone when the alarms went off."

"Does she have a back-up clone?"

"There isn't time to discuss that now. The plane is ready to go, and we should get out of here before those reporters or the police start asking you questions. Come with me to my car. I'll give Harriman a call and let him know we're on our way."

They went around the side of the building, got into Simpson's car and drove past the fire trucks.

"I can't stay away too long," said Simpson as they drove through the security gate. "The police still want to talk to someone in charge. And since Pender isn't here, I'll need to get back to do damage control."

Harriman was standing next to a LennoxGen limousine when Simpson pulled onto the airport tarmac and rolled down his window.

"How's Lennox doing?" Simpson asked.

"He's not talking very much. I've got him waiting in the hangar. The pilot's not here yet."

"Here," Simpson said, handing Harriman a bottle of pills. "Make sure he takes one of these. I've got Zenden here. He's more stable, but he'll also need to take a dose in a couple of hours. You'll have to go with them to Zurich. Here are their travel documents." He reached into a briefcase and gave Harriman a folder. "I need to get back to the main facility. The police are asking a lot of questions. How long before the pilot arrives?"

"Fifteen minutes at the most, but I haven't got my passport. I'll have to go home and get it."

"How long will that take?"

"Half an hour or so. Is it OK to leave Lennox and Zenden alone?"

"I'd better wait here until the pilot arrives," said Simpson.

"That won't be necessary," Luke said, getting out of the car and walking over to Harriman. "Give me the medicine, and I'll make sure Lennox takes it. I'm sure we'll both be fine until the pilot gets here."

"Excellent," Simpson said. "Call me on the sky phone once you're airborne."

"I will," Luke said, taking the medicine from Harriman, who got into the limousine and drove off, followed by Simpson.

As soon as they were out of sight, Luke threw the pills as far away as he could. Then he turned and walked toward the hangar.

14
Personality Clash

A plane emblazoned with the LennoxGen logo stood inside the hangar. Luke headed for a small office in the far corner. The door was open, and Patrick was pacing the floor. He stopped when he spotted Luke in the doorway.

"Cornelius!" Patrick exclaimed, "I'm glad your download was a success."

"Not exactly," said Luke. "Zenden didn't make it."

"You?"

"That's right, and you won't make it either because I've thrown your pills away."

"Idiot!" he snapped. "Do you think a child can stop all this? This is much bigger than you can ever imagine," he said, grabbing a nearby wrench.

Luke stood his ground and watched as Patrick's grip tightened around the wrench. Luke thought about the fights he and Patrick had had over the years at the gym. Patrick had always been bigger and stronger, but now Luke wasn't just fighting his old friend. Lennox was in control of Patrick's body and would be doing his utmost to kill him.

Patrick's eyes narrowed. Luke met his icy stare, and the two boys stood like statues facing each other. Patrick shifted his weight from one foot to the other, then suddenly swung the wrench wildly at Luke. It narrowly missed Luke's head, and he staggered backwards out of the office. Patrick charged clumsily after him.

Lennox doesn't know any karate moves, Luke suddenly realized, shifting his weight and knocking the wrench out of Patrick's hand.

But Patrick managed to grab Luke's arm, forcing him against the plane. For a split second, Luke thought he saw a glimmer of recognition in Patrick's eyes.

"Luke?" asked Patrick, furrowing his brow. His grip relaxed just enough for Luke to kick him sharply in the shin. Patrick cursed and let him go.

When Luke looked into Patrick's eyes now, all he saw was sheer hate.

"This body is mine," Patrick sneered. But then his face contorted in pain and anguish as a confrontation between Lennox and Patrick began in earnest.

"Patrick is weak! I will survive!"

While Luke watched, Patrick staggered around the hangar, clutching the sides of his head in agony.

"No! No!" he screeched. "I must survive!"

Then, with an ear-splitting scream, Patrick charged. But Luke easily grabbed his arm, bent it backwards and forced Patrick to the ground with a thud. Patrick's expression went blank, and his eyes rolled back in their sockets.

"Patrick!" exclaimed Luke. "Are you OK?"

Patrick's eyes flickered, then opened wide. "Is it over?" gasped Patrick. "Is Lennox gone?"

"I think so," said Luke guardedly.

Luke helped Patrick up as the sound of an approaching car could be heard.

"That might be Harriman," Luke said. "Hide in the office. I'll take care of him."

15 Headline News

Five days later, Luke stood on the Ericksons' front porch.

"Hi, Luke," Emma said, opening the door. "Mom's over at the hospital visiting Patrick. Come on in."

Luke followed her into the kitchen. "I know. I was just leaving him when she arrived."

"How's he doing today?"

"He couldn't talk much, but the nurse said he's getting better. How are you feeling?"

"I'm fine," she said, sitting down at the table. "It was really weird, though. You dragged me away just in time. I felt as if I were a prisoner in my own body. I could feel my muscles moving and heard echoes of someone else's thoughts inside my head."

"Sounds pretty weird," said Luke.

"It was like listening to people talking on the surface when you're underwater. Sometimes I'd suddenly come up for air, but then just as quickly I'd plunge back into the blackness again. I can't imagine what it must have been like for Patrick. Lennox had control of him for so much longer. I still have a headache, but it's not bad, considering all that's happened."

Emma reached behind her and handed Luke an envelope. "Here's the letter that came this morning from Lisa."

Luke quickly scanned it.

Hi, Luke and Emma,

I hope you're both doing OK and keeping a low profile. I phoned the hospital to check on Patrick and they tell me he's doing fine. Make sure you watch Nathaniel Benson tonight at six.

Lisa

"Hey," said Luke, looking at his watch. "We better turn it on now."

Emma grabbed the remote and switched the TV on. The news had already started.

"The fire destroyed much of the company's pioneering work in genetics, which will be a major blow to infertility treatment around the globe. There were four fatalities, but most of the staff escaped the blaze without serious injury. We spoke earlier with the company's former public relations director."

"It's Lisa," said Luke.

*"Miss MacKenzie, there are rumours
that LennoxGen is involved in human
cloning."*

*"That's correct. There is now a wide-
ranging international investigation
into LennoxGen. I'm afraid I'm
unable to add any further comments,
as legal proceedings are pending,
and I am a material witness against
the company."*

Nathaniel Benson turned to face the camera.

*"There have already been a number
of arrests in the case. A local police
inspector was just placed in custody
this afternoon."*

"Look, it's Tremaine!" Emma exclaimed.

A stern-faced Roberta Tremaine appeared on
the TV, flanked by two police officers. She was
quickly ushered into the rear seat of a waiting
patrol car.

"Today in sports..."

Emma switched the TV off and turned toward Luke. "You never told me how you and Patrick got away from the airport."

"It was easy," Luke grinned. "The pilot arrived to collect Rupert Lennox and Cornelius Zenden, but all he found were two kids who were lost. I got him to drive us both home."